Peter Pan
and Wendy

★ *For my dear friend Jane* ★
R. I.

★ *For Lily* ★
I. B.

Also by Rose Impey and Ian Beck
THE ORCHARD BOOK OF FAIRY TALES

ORCHARD BOOKS
96 Leonard Street
London EC2A 4RH
Orchard Books Australia
14 Mars Road, Lane Cove, NSW 2066
First published in Great Britain 1998
Illustrations © Ian Beck 1998
Text, this edition © Rose Impey 1998
Peter Pan © Great Ormond Street Children's Hospital, London 1937
The right of Ian Beck to be identified as the Illustrator and
Rose Impey as the Author of this Work has been asserted
by them in accordance with the Copyright, Designs and Patents Act, 1988.
A CIP catalogue record for the book is available from the British Library.
Printed in Dubai

ISBN 1-86039-381-0

J. M. Barrie's

Peter Pan and Wendy

Adapted by Rose Impey
Pictures by Ian Beck

ORCHARD BOOKS

CONTENTS

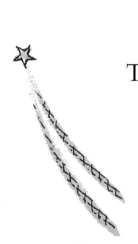

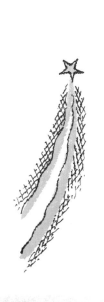

PETER PAN AND THE HOSPITAL FOR SICK CHILDREN, GREAT ORMOND STREET

J.M. Barrie had no children of his own yet he created a classic story which has been enjoyed by each new generation of children for nearly a hundred years. Every year *Peter Pan* is performed at theatres all over the world and it has become part of childhood tradition.

Inspired by the imaginative games of the small sons of a family friend, J.M. Barrie told them wonderful stories of pirates and islands which eventually became part of *Peter Pan*. It was first performed as a play at the Duke of York Theatre in London in 1904, and in 1911 *Peter Pan and Wendy* was first published as a full-length story.

In 1929 J.M. Barrie generously donated all the rights in *Peter Pan* to the Hospital for Sick Children, Great Ormond Street, a bequest which continued after his death in 1937. In 1988 an Act of Parliament granted these rights in perpetuity so that the Hospital would continue to benefit from the royalties. A royalty on this edition will therefore also be paid to the Hospital.

One

WHO IS PETER PAN?

All children grow up, all except one. This is the story of that one – Peter Pan – and of the little girl – Wendy Moira Angela Darling – who nearly didn't…

Wendy lived at Number 14 with her family: her father and mother, Mr and Mrs Darling, and her two brothers, John and Michael. Mrs Darling was a lovely lady and the chief person in the house, although Mr Darling liked to think he was. Mr Darling worked in the city and knew about difficult things like stocks and shares. There was a maid called Liza and a nurse for the children called Nana.

In every way they were a perfectly respectable family, except for the fact that Nana was a dog.

But, as strange as that might sound, Nana was a treasure of a nurse. Her kennel was kept in the nursery, so she could be up at any moment in the night if one of the children made the slightest cry. She knew exactly when a cough was a thing to have no patience with and when it needed a stocking round your throat, and she believed in old-fashioned remedies like rhubarb leaf; Nana had no time for new-fangled talk about germs!

Every day Nana led the children to school, carrying an umbrella in her mouth in case it rained, and then waited with the other nurses to take the children home. The other nurses sat on benches to wait, of course, while Nana lay on the floor, but that was the only difference.

No nursery could possibly have been organised better, and Mr Darling knew it, but he sometimes wondered uneasily whether the neighbours talked about them.

He also had a suspicion that Nana didn't respect him as she ought to. But really there never was a more contented family – until the coming of Peter Pan.

Mrs Darling first heard of Peter when she was tidying up her children's minds. It is the nightly custom of every good mother, after her children are asleep, to rummage through their minds and put things straight for next morning. It's rather like tidying up drawers. She would fold up their naughty thoughts and tuck them away at the bottom of their minds; and lay out neatly on top all their prettier thoughts, ready for them to put on when they wake. This was how she came to discover the Neverland, the make-believe island on which the children played.

Now, although it was the same island, each of the children imagined it differently: John imagined a lagoon with flamingos flying over it, while Michael, who was very small, had a flamingo with lagoons flying over it. John lived in an upturned boat, Michael in a wigwam and Wendy, with her own pet wolf, in a house of leaves sewn together. Sometimes their islands got mixed up, never jumbled though, just nicely crammed with adventures.

Occasionally Mrs Darling found things in her children's minds she couldn't understand: the word Peter for instance. She knew no one called Peter. Here it was in John's mind, then Michael's; then she found it scrawled all over Wendy's. And always it had a rather cheeky appearance.

"Yes, he is rather cheeky," Wendy admitted. "He is Peter Pan, you know, Mother."

Mrs Darling could just remember from her own childhood a Peter Pan who was said to live with the fairies. But surely he wasn't real?

"Oh, yes he is," Wendy assured her. She told her mother how he came into the nursery at night and sat on the foot of her bed and played his pipes while she was asleep. She even showed her mother the leaves he had left on the floor by the window where he had not wiped his feet.

Mrs Darling didn't know what to think. How could anyone have got in? They were three floors up and it was thirty feet to the pavement without so much as a spout to climb up by. Wendy must have been dreaming, she told herself.

But Wendy had not been dreaming, as Mrs Darling discovered the very next night.

It happened to be Nana's evening off and Mrs Darling was sitting in the nursery, sewing. The children were asleep, the fire was warm and Mrs Darling's head began to nod. She dreamt that the Neverland had come too close and that a strange boy had broken through from it. As she dreamed, the nursery window blew open and a boy did drop on the floor. He was accompanied by a strange light which darted about the room like a living thing.

It was this light that woke Mrs Darling.

She started up with a cry; she knew at once that the boy was Peter Pan and when Peter saw she was a grown-up, he gnashed his little teeth at her.

Mrs Darling screamed and Nana, returning from her evening out, rushed in. She sprang at the boy, who leapt lightly through the window, but Nana slammed the window shut, trapping his shadow in it.

It was quite an ordinary kind of shadow. Mrs Darling thought of showing it to her husband, but he was busy doing sums: totting up the cost of winter coats for John and Michael with a wet towel round his head to keep his brain clear; it seemed a shame to disturb him.

Besides, Mrs Darling knew exactly what he would say, just as he had said before when she'd mentioned Peter Pan: "This all comes of having a dog for a nurse. It's no doubt some nonsense Nana has been putting into their heads. Leave it alone and it will all blow over."

So Mrs Darling rolled up the shadow and put it away carefully in a drawer.

But the matter did not blow over. Oh, dear me, no.

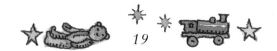

Two

THAT NEVER-TO-BE-FORGOTTEN
FRIDAY EVENING

A week later, on a Friday evening, Mr and Mrs Darling were getting ready to go out to dinner at Number 27.

Nana was putting on the water for Michael's bath and carrying him to it on her back. Michael was creating quite a fuss. "It isn't six o'clock yet. I won't go to bed!" he shouted. "Nana, I tell you I won't be bathed, I won't, I won't." But of course he was.

Then Mrs Darling had come in, wearing her white evening gown, and Wendy and John had stopped their game to admire her. It was then that Mr Darling had rushed in, in an awful temper, carrying a crumpled tie in his hand. Mr Darling was rather given to tempers, because although he could do all sorts of difficult things like sums, simple things would often catch him out.

"Why, what is the matter, my dear?" asked Mrs Darling.

"Matter!" he yelled. "This tie is the matter! It will not tie. Not round my neck! Round the bedpost, oh, yes, twenty times I have tied it round the bedpost, but round my neck, no! Oh, dear no! It begs to be excused!"

"Let me try," said Mrs Darling calmly, and in moments she had tied it perfectly.

Immediately Mr Darling's temper was restored and he was soon dancing round the room with Michael on his back.

But unluckily Nana came in, in the middle of the game, and brushed against Mr Darling's new black trousers covering them with dog hairs, and off he went into a second temper. "Haven't I always said what a mistake it is to have a dog for a nurse?" he shouted.

Now Mrs Darling knew what a treasure Nana was and, since the coming of Peter Pan, she felt much safer leaving the children in her care. She thought this was the moment to show her husband the boy's shadow.

Mr Darling was puzzled. "It's nobody I know," he said, examining it carefully, "but he does look a scoundrel."

They were still discussing it when Nana came in with Michael's medicine; Michael refused to take it and another commotion began. Mrs Darling left the room to get Michael a chocolate.

"Don't mollycoddle him," his father called after her. "Be a man, Michael."

"Won't, won't," Michael cried naughtily.

"Why, when I was your age I took medicine without a murmur."

Mr Darling really believed this was true, and so did Wendy. "That medicine that you sometimes take, Father, is much nastier, isn't it?" she said.

"Ever so much nastier," Mr Darling said bravely, "and I would take it now as an example to you, Michael, if I hadn't lost the bottle."

In fact he hadn't exactly lost it; he had climbed up in the dead of night and hidden it on top of the wardrobe. What he didn't know was that Liza, the maid, had found it. Wendy knew just where she had put it and brought it in a moment.

Now Mr Darling was trapped. "Michael first," he said doggedly.

"Father first," said Michael.

Mr Darling was sure he would be sick and still refused.

"Father's a cowardy custard," said Michael, and the two of them continued to quarrel until Wendy suggested, "Why not both take it at the same time? One, two, three..."

Michael took his honourably, but Mr Darling slipped his behind his back.

"Oh, Father!" Wendy exclaimed. The children looked at him reproachfully.

"Look here," he said, trying to get round them. "I've just thought of a splendid joke."

He poured his medicine, which was the colour of milk, into Nana's bowl and when she came in the poor dog wagged her tail and innocently lapped it up. Then she gave her master such a look. Mr Darling felt quite ashamed of himself, which sent him into the third temper of the evening.

"It was only a joke!" he roared.

But Mrs Darling, when she returned, was not amused either. She comforted the boys, while Wendy hugged Nana.

"That's right," shouted their father. "Spoil her! Nobody spoils me. Oh, dear no! I'm only the breadwinner, why should I be spoiled? Well, I refuse to allow that dog to rule this nursery for an hour longer." He took hold of Nana's collar and led her out. "The proper place for you is in the yard, and that's where you'll go to be tied up this instant."

The children wept, but their father would not be persuaded and Mrs Darling put them to bed in unhappy silence. They could hear Nana barking down below.

"She's barking because Father's chaining her up in the yard," said John.

But Wendy knew better. "That isn't Nana's unhappy

bark, that's her bark when she smells danger."

Mrs Darling was just then lighting their night-lights and a nameless fear clutched at her heart and made her cry out, "Oh, how I wish I wasn't going to a party tonight!"

Then Michael asked, "Can anything harm us, Mother, after the night-lights are lit?"

"Nothing, precious," she said, reassuring them. "They are the eyes a mother leaves behind her to guard her children."

As she kissed the children goodnight, all the stars in the night sky seemed to crowd round the house, curious to see what would happen next. As a rule the stars are not really friendly to Peter Pan, who has a mischievous way of trying to blow them out, but they are so fond of fun, the little ones especially, that they were on Peter's side tonight.

The moment Mr and Mrs Darling had left the house, picking their way through the snow, the brightest of all the stars screamed out, "Now, Peter!"

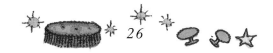

Three

THE ARRIVAL OF PETER PAN

Moments later the children's night-lights yawned, blinked and went out. But the room was soon lit by another light a thousand times brighter. The light was a tiny fairy, called Tinker Bell; she was searching every corner of the nursery, looking for Peter's shadow. Peter followed her into the room. He had carried her part of the way and his hand was covered with fairy dust. They found his shadow in a drawer and, in his delight to recover it, Peter didn't notice that he had shut Tinker Bell inside.

He sat on the carpet and tried every way he could think of to stick his shadow back on; he even tried soap. When that didn't work he started to cry; his sobs woke Wendy.

"Why are you crying?" she said.

Peter stopped crying and politely asked, "What's your name?"

"Wendy Moira Angela Darling," said Wendy. "What's yours?"

"Peter Pan."

"And where do you live?"

"Second to the right and then straight on till morning."

"What a funny address!" she said.

"No, it isn't," said Peter sharply.

"I only mean," Wendy explained, "is that what they put on your letters?"

"Don't get any letters," he said.

"But your mother gets letters?"

"Don't have a mother." Nor did Peter want one; he thought them very overrated persons.

But Wendy felt sorry on his behalf. "Oh, Peter, no wonder you were crying."

"I wasn't crying about mothers," he said. "I was crying because I can't get my shadow to stick on. Besides I wasn't crying."

Wendy smiled when she saw that Peter had been trying to stick his shadow on with soap. How exactly like a boy, she thought. She quickly found her sewing basket and offered to sew it on for him. "I dare say it will hurt a little," she warned him.

"I shan't cry," said Peter, clenching his teeth.

Soon his shadow was behaving properly and Peter was jumping about in delight. "How clever I am," he crowed, just as if he'd attached the shadow himself.

Wendy was shocked to see how conceited Peter was. She went back to bed and refused to speak to him. But Peter could be very charming. "Oh, Wendy, don't be cross, one girl is more use than twenty boys," he told her.

"Do you really think so?" said Wendy, immediately forgiving him. She even offered him a kiss. Peter held out his hand for it.

"Surely you know what a kiss is," said Wendy, shocked.

"I shall when you give it to me," he replied.

So, rather than hurt his feelings, she handed him a thimble. Peter politely gave her a kiss back; he dropped an acorn in her hand. Wendy smiled and said she would wear it on a chain round her neck.

It was lucky that she did, for it was afterwards to save her life.

"How old are you, Peter?" Wendy asked him.

Peter wasn't at all sure. "You see, Wendy, I ran away the day I was born. I heard my mother and father talking about what I was to be when I became a man. I don't want ever to be a man," he said with passion. "I want always to be a little boy and to have fun. So I ran away to live in Kensington Gardens, among the fairies."

Then Peter explained to Wendy how fairies began.

"When the first baby laughed, its laugh broke into a thousand pieces, and they all went skipping about, and that was the beginning of fairies. But children know such a lot now," he told her, "they soon don't believe in fairies, and every time a child says, 'I don't believe in fairies', a fairy somewhere dies."

Suddenly with all this talk of fairies Peter realised how quiet Tinker Bell was being. He called out to her and the tiniest tinkle of bells came from the chest of drawers.

"I do believe I shut her up in the drawer," Peter said grinning.

He let Tink out and she flew about the nursery screaming with fury in her fairy language. When she finally stopped still for a moment, Wendy caught sight of her.

"Oh, she's lovely," she said. But Tink didn't return the compliment.

Peter translated for Wendy. "She says you are a great ugly girl. She's not very polite, I'm afraid."

Peter and Wendy sat cosily together in the armchair.

"Where do you live?" Wendy asked Peter.

"With the lost boys," he told her. "They are the children who fall out of their prams. If they are not claimed in seven days they are sent away to the Neverland and I am the captain. Only there are no girls," Peter added cunningly. "Girls are much too clever to fall out of their prams."

"I think it's perfectly lovely the way you talk about girls," said Wendy. And this time she gave Peter a proper kiss. Immediately Wendy began to squeal. Someone was pulling her hair. I'm afraid Tinker Bell was rather jealous of Wendy; she didn't want to share Peter with anyone. Wendy, for her part, was disappointed to learn that Peter didn't come to the nursery window especially to see her, but to listen to stories.

"Oh, Wendy, your mother was telling such a lovely story about the prince who couldn't find the lady who wore the glass slipper."

"That was Cinderella," said Wendy excitedly, "and he found her, and they lived happily ever after."

Peter jumped up and rushed to the window.

"Oh, please don't go," she begged him. "I know lots more stories."

"Wendy, come with me and tell them to the other boys," said Peter. "You could tuck us in at night, and darn our clothes, and make pockets for us. None of us has pockets. You could be our mother. We should all love you."

Wendy could hardly resist him, but then she thought of leaving her own mother. "Besides, I can't fly," she said.

"I'll teach you."

"And John and Michael too?"

"If you like," he said carelessly; and she jumped out of bed and shook her brothers. "Wake up!" she cried. "Peter Pan has come and he is going to teach us to fly."

The boys were awake in a moment: Michael looking as sharp as a knife with six blades and a saw, and John alert to the first sound of footsteps on the stairs.

"Out with the light! Hide! Quick!" he cried, so that when Liza came in, holding Nana on the lead, the nursery was silent. The children were cleverly pretending to sleep.

"There, you suspicious brute," she said, "they're perfectly safe. Every one of the little angels sound asleep and breathing."

But Nana knew that kind of breathing. She tried to drag herself free but Liza pulled her out of the room and tied her up in the yard again. Nana was determined to raise the

alarm. She strained and strained at her chain until at last she broke it. In a matter of minutes she had burst into the dining room of Number 27 and flung up her paws, begging her master and mistress to come home immediately.

But those few minutes had given Peter Pan the time he needed to work his magic on the children. He showed them how to fly round the room. First they tried from the floor and then from their beds, but they always went down instead of up.

"Think lovely thoughts," he said. "They will lift you into the air."

But they didn't, at least not until he blew a little of the fairy dust from his hands on to each of them. Then all three children rose up, their heads bobbing against the ceiling.

"I flewed," cried Michael.

"Look at me! Look at me!" they squealed in delight.

The cunning Peter led them closer to the open window. The boys followed; only Wendy hesitated, but Peter whispered in her ear, "Mermaids," and "Pirates," he told the boys.

"Pirates!" cried John, seizing his Sunday hat. "Let us go at once."

At that very moment, Mr and Mrs Darling crossed the street and looked up at the nursery window. The room was ablaze with light and they could see in shadow three figures circling round the room, not on the floor but in the air.

Not three figures, but four!

Their hearts almost bursting, they raced into the house. But, when Mr and Mrs Darling reached the nursery, they were too late. The birds had already flown.

Four

THE FLIGHT TO NEVERLAND

"Second to the right, and straight on till morning."

That, Peter told Wendy, was the way to the Neverland.

They flew for a long time, although none of them knew for how long, bumping into clouds on the way. Sometimes it was dark and sometimes light, now they were very cold and then too warm. Sometimes they were sleepy and then down fell one of the boys.

Unlike Peter they couldn't sleep in the air without falling. Luckily Peter was there to save them. But he so liked to tease Wendy that he always waited till the last moment, diving through the air to catch them before they could strike the sea. At last they drew near Neverland.

They reached it not so much thanks to Peter's guidance, as because the island was out looking for them, which is the only way to find those magic shores.

"There it is," said Peter calmly.

"Where, where?" Wendy, John and Michael stood on tiptoe in the air to get their first sight of it and, strange to say, they recognised it at once.

They spotted John's flamingo and Michael's cave and Wendy's pet wolf. Peter was a little annoyed with them for knowing so much, but when the island began to look dark and threatening and fear fell upon them, they were glad to draw close to him, especially when he showed them a pirate asleep in the grass.

"If you like we'll go down and capture him," he offered.

"Suppose he were to wake up," said John.

Peter was indignant. "You don't think I would attack him while he was sleeping, do you?"

"Are there many pirates on the island just now?" John asked.

"Never known so many," said Peter. "And the worst of the lot is Hook."

"Captain Hook?" said the children trembling, for they had heard of Hook's reputation.

"Don't worry, he's not as big as he was," Peter boasted. "I cut off a bit of him."

"Which bit?" asked John.

"His right hand."

"Oh, then he can't fight now?" said John, relieved.

"Oh, can't he though! He has an iron hook and he claws with it. But there's one thing you must promise," said Peter, "if we meet Hook in open fight, you must leave him to me."

"I promise," John said loyally.

Peter had sent Tinker Bell ahead but now she circled back to warn them that the pirates had sighted them and got out their big gun, Long Tom. When the children realised that Tink's light might help the pirates spot them, they begged Peter to send her away. But Peter refused to send Tink away by herself when she was frightened. Instead he persuaded her to travel in John's hat. Wendy carried it, which, as you'll see in a little while, led to mischief.

Tink, you know, was not all bad: just now she was all bad, but sometimes she was all good. Fairies, being so small, have room for one feeling only at a time. Now she was full of jealousy of Wendy.

Suddenly the air was broken by a tremendous crash; the pirates had fired Long Tom. The children became separated, hurled in different directions. It would have been better then for Wendy if she had dropped the hat. Instead she trusted Tinker Bell and followed her to her doom.

Meanwhile on the island, sensing that Peter was on his way back, everyone had begun to liven up. The lost boys were out at that moment looking for Peter, the pirates were out looking for the lost boys, the redskins were out looking for the pirates, and the beasts were out looking for the redskins. They were all circling the island, but they didn't meet up because all were moving in the same direction.

First in the procession came Tootles, a sweet, sad boy who always suffered from bad luck, then Nibs, who was much more cheerful. Next came Slightly who could remember a little of his earlier life before he was lost. This tended to make him conceited, although not as conceited as Peter. Next came Curly, who got into scrapes, and finally the Twins, who nobody, not even Peter, could tell apart.

The boys moved on and after a pause came the pirates on their track, singing their dreadful song:

"Avast belay, yo ho, heave to,
A-pirating we go,
And if we're parted by a shot
We're sure to meet below!"

A more villainous-looking lot you are never likely to meet. There were far too many to name all of them, so let us pick just two: the Irish bo'sun Smee, a kindly-looking man but all the more dangerous for that, and Starkey, sometimes called Gentleman Starkey. And then, the worst of the lot, James Hook, cruel and clever, with perfect manners. Indeed, the more cunning Hook became the more polite he grew. There was only one thing Hook feared in the whole world and that was the sight of his own blood.

Next, on the trail of the pirates, came the redskins, armed with tomahawks and knives. Leading his braves was Great Big Little Panther, with his daughter, the beautiful Tiger Lily, bringing up the rear.

Then, as the redskins disappeared like shadows, the beasts followed close behind: lions, tigers, bears and other smaller savage creatures, their tongues hanging out; hungry as usual.

And, last of all, a gigantic crocodile. We shall see presently for whom it was searching.

The procession continued to circle the island, for some time each of the parties keeping a sharp look out in the front, none of them suspecting that danger might be creeping up from behind.

But at last the lost boys approached their home and threw themselves on the ground, talking of Peter. "I do wish he would come home," said Slightly, "and tell us whether he has heard anything more about Cinderella."

Suddenly there was a sound the boys knew only too well
– the pirates were approaching. In a flash the boys were
gone, into their underground home. Rabbits couldn't have
disappeared more quickly. But Nibs stayed behind and
slipped into the woods.

Starkey saw him and raised his gun.

"Put back that pistol," snarled Hook. "D'you want to lose
your scalp? Tiger Lily's redskins will be upon us. He is only
one; I want all seven. Now, scatter and look for them."

The pirates disappeared among the trees. The captain sat
down on a large mushroom and began to confide in his
faithful bo'sun.

"Most of all, Smee, I want Peter Pan. 'Twas he cut off my
arm and flung it to a passing crocodile. It liked my arm so
much it has followed me ever since, licking its lips for the
rest of me. That crocodile would have had me before now,
but by chance it swallowed a clock which goes tick-tick-tick

inside it, so before it can reach me I hear the tick and run."

"Some day that clock will stop, Captain," said Smee, "and then it'll get you."

"Aye, that's the fear that haunts me. Odds bobs, hammer and tongs, I'm burning," yelled the captain jumping up. "This seat is hot."

The pirates had discovered the chimney to the boys' underground home, and when they pulled it away, and heard the boys talking below, they made an even more important discovery.

A curdling smile lit up Hook's cruel face. "So Peter Pan is away, is he? Let us return to the ship. I have a plan to cook a

large rich cake and leave it for these silly boys. Having no mother they will not know how dangerous it is to eat rich damp cake. Aha, they will die!"

Smee was filled with admiration and the two pirates began to dance and sing, until a familiar sound broke in: tick-tick-tick...

"The crocodile," gasped Hook and bounded away with Smee hot on his heels and the crocodile oozing after them.

A little later, when the boys emerged from their underground home, Nibs rushed breathless into their midst.

"I've seen a wonderful thing," he cried. "A great white bird, flying this way."

"What kind of bird?"

"I don't know, but as it flies it moans 'Poor Wendy'."

"I remember those," said Slightly. "There are birds called Wendies."

Wendy was now almost overhead and they could hear her cry. But louder still they could hear Tinker Bell's shrill voice telling them, "Peter wants you to shoot the Wendy."

It was not in the boys' nature to question Peter's orders; they raced to get their bows and arrows, but Tootles, unlucky boy, had his already to hand.

"Quick, Tootles," Tink screamed. "Peter will be so pleased."

Tootles lifted his bow and fired and Wendy fluttered to the ground with an arrow in her breast.

Five

THE LITTLE HOUSE

When the other boys returned, armed with their bows and arrows, they found Tootles alone, standing over the body. Tinker Bell had flown away and hidden herself.

"I have shot the Wendy," Tootles cried proudly.

But a terrible silence fell upon the wood.

"This is no bird," said Slightly in a scared voice. "I think it's a lady."

"A lady to take care of us at last," said one of the twins, "and Tootles has killed her."

It was at this tragic moment that they heard a sound which made the heart of every one of them rise to his mouth. They heard Peter crow.

The frightened boys quickly tried to hide Wendy as Peter dropped in front of them.

"Great news," he cried. "I've brought a mother for you all. She flew this way. Have you not seen her?"

The other boys would still have hidden her, but Tootles made them stand back and let Peter see. For once Peter didn't know what to do. "She is dead," he said uncomfortably. Then he demanded sternly, "Whose arrow?"

"Mine, Peter," said Tootles. Peter took the arrow and made to stab Tootles with it, but something stopped him.

Wendy raised her arm. "Poor Tootles," she whispered.

"She lives," said Peter, and kneeling beside her he found the acorn he had given her. The arrow had struck against it. "See, it's the kiss. It saved her life." Peter begged Wendy to get better, but she was still in a deep faint.

When Peter learned that it was Tink who had told the boys to shoot at Wendy, they had never seen him more angry. "I am your friend no more," he told her. "Be gone for ever." But when Wendy again raised her arm he relented. "Well, not for ever, but for a whole week."

Now they turned their attention to what they should do with Wendy until she was fully recovered. Peter had the delightful idea of building a house around her, where she lay. In a moment the boys were scurrying this way and that, bringing everything that was needed. Then who should appear but John and Michael; they had at last found their way. They were curious to see all this activity.

"Who's the house for?" they wondered.

"For the Wendy," said Curly.

"For Wendy?" said John, aghast. "Why, she's only a girl."

But, on Peter's orders, the two boys were dragged off to help.

The house was soon looking quite beautiful. Peter strode up and down, inspecting it.

First there was no knocker, so Tootles offered the sole of his shoe, and then no chimney. Peter snatched the hat off John's head, knocked out the bottom, and put the hat on the roof. The little house seemed so pleased to have such a capital chimney that smoke immediately began to come out of the hat.

When it was really and truly finished, they knocked on

the door which opened and Wendy came out.

"What a lovely, darling house," she said, which were the very words they had hoped she would say.

The boys went on their knees and begged Wendy to be their mother.

For a moment she hesitated. "I'm only a little girl. I have no real experience."

But Peter assured her, "What we need is just a nice motherly person."

"Very well," she said. "Come inside at once, you naughty children; I'm sure your feet are damp. And before I put you to bed we've just time to finish the story of Cinderella."

So in they went and that was only the first of many joyous evenings they spent together.

Once Wendy was completely recovered, Peter thought it safer for them all to live in the home underground. The first thing to do was to measure the children for their own hollow trees. It was one of Peter's cleverer ideas that each of them should have their own entrance which fitted them perfectly. Unless your tree fitted you, you couldn't go up and down it. Once you fitted, you simply drew in your breath at the top, and down you went at exactly the right speed, while to go up you drew in and let out, drew in and let out, and this way you wriggled up. After a few days' practice they could all go up and down as easily as buckets in a well.

The house underground consisted of one large room. Growing in it were stout mushrooms which they used as stools. In the middle of the floor a Never tree tried its best to grow, but every morning they sawed it off, level with the floor, so that by tea-time it was the perfect height, with a door on top of it, to make a table. The bed was leant against the wall by day, and let down at six-thirty; and all the boys except Michael slept in it, like sardines in a tin. But Wendy insisted on there being a baby, and, since Michael was the littlest, he was hung up to sleep in a basket.

There was one small recess in the wall which was
Tinker Bell's apartment, shut off from the rest by a tiny
curtain.

It was a charming life for Wendy, looking after her
children, cooking their meals and darning their socks.
No one ever knew exactly whether there would be a
real meal or whether it would be just make-believe; it
all depended on Peter. Make-believe was so real to him
that during a meal of it you actually could see him
getting fatter.

Wendy's favourite time for sewing and darning was after her children had all gone to bed. You might think this was the time when she would miss her beloved parents, but I don't think she did. Of course she thought of them; and then she was absolutely confident that they would always keep the window open for her to fly back by.

But mainly the children were far too busy having adventures to think a great deal about home. Sometimes Peter went off alone having adventures on his own, but there were many more adventures he shared with the others. You would need a much longer book than this to tell them all, but let's choose one at least. Now, which one shall it be?

Six

ADVENTURE ON MAROONERS' ROCK

One of the children's favourite places was the Mermaids' Lagoon. Here they spent long summer days, swimming or floating, watching the mermaids' games. Don't imagine from this that the mermaids were on friendly terms with the children; on the contrary, it was among Wendy's lasting regrets that all the time she was on the island she never had a kind word from one of them. Only Peter was allowed to come close; he sat by the hour chatting with them on Marooners' Rock, while the mermaids lazily combed out their hair.

On this particular day the children were lying on the rock, stretched out in the sun, sleeping off their make-believe lunch, when a change came over the lagoon.

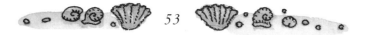

It was not that night had come, but something as dark as
night had sent a shiver through the sea to say that it was
coming. There was the sound of muffled oars. A boat was on
its way.

Peter, who could sniff danger even in his sleep, sprang up
and roused the others. "Pirates!" he cried. "Dive!"

There was a gleam of legs, and instantly the lagoon
seemed deserted. The pirates' dinghy, with three figures in it,
drew nearer, and in the gloom crashed into the rock.

"Luff, you lubber," cried Smee. "Now then, let's hoist the
redskin on to this rock and leave her there. When the tide
rises she will drown."

Starkey helped lift out the beautiful Tiger Lily. She had
been caught boarding the pirate ship with a knife in her
mouth. On Hook's orders she had been bound hand and
foot and brought here to her watery doom.

Peter and Wendy watched, bobbing up and down in the
water close by. Peter was determined to save Tiger Lily.
"Ahoy, there, you lubbers," he cried in the voice of Captain
Hook. It was such a marvellous imitation that the pirates
looked out, expecting to see their captain swimming towards
them.

"We're putting the redskin on the rock, Captain," Smee
called out.

"Set her free," came the astonishing answer.

"Free!"

"Yes, cut her bonds and let her go, or I'll plunge my hook in you."

The pirates knew better than to risk their captain's anger. They cut Tiger Lily free and she slid like an eel into the water.

But a minute later the real Hook's voice rang out over the lagoon, "Boat ahoy!"

His hook gripped the side of the boat and he hauled himself aboard, dripping with water. He sat with his head on his hook looking profoundly unhappy.

"Captain, is all well?" his men asked timidly.

"The game's up," he sighed. "Those boys have found a mother."

"What's a mother?" asked the ignorant Smee.

Wendy was so shocked that she burst out, "He doesn't know!"

Peter pulled her beneath the water just as the pirates looked out to see who had spoken. All they saw was a nest floating on the lagoon and sitting on it was the Never bird. It had built in a tree overhanging the lagoon and when the nest had fallen into the water, the bird continued to sit on her eggs. On Peter's orders she was never to be disturbed.

"That," said Hook bitterly, "is a mother. See, lads, a mother would never desert her eggs. What a lesson!"

Smee was much impressed. "Captain, could we not kidnap the boys' mother and make her ours?"

"It's a princely scheme," cried Hook. "We'll seize the children and carry them to the boat: the boys we'll make walk the plank, but Wendy shall be our mother."

Once more Wendy could not contain herself. "Never!" she cried, bobbing under the water.

But it was then that Hook remembered Tiger Lily. "Where is the redskin?" he demanded abruptly.

The pirates were surprised. "We let her go," answered Smee, "on your orders."

"I gave no such order," said Hook, shaking a little. Something strange was afoot. He cried out. "Spirit that haunts this dark lagoon, do you hear me?"

"Odds bobs, hammer and tongs, I hear you," Peter answered in Hook's voice.

"Who are you, stranger?" Hook demanded. "Speak to me!"

"I am James Hook," replied the voice, "captain of the Jolly Roger."

"But if you are Hook," said the pirate almost humbly, "tell me who am I?"

"A codfish," replied the voice.

"A codfish!" Hook echoed. His men looked at him with new eyes. Had they been captained all this time by a codfish?

Hook suddenly tried a guessing game. "Are you a man?"

"No!" the answer rang out scornfully.

"Boy?"

"Yes."

"Ordinary boy?"

"No!"

"Wonderful boy?"

"Yes! I am…Peter Pan."

"Pan! Now we have him," Hook shouted. "Into the water. Take him dead or alive."

At the same time came the real voice of Peter Pan. "Are you ready, boys?"

Answers came from all parts of the lagoon and the fighting began. It was short and sharp. John gallantly climbed into the boat and struggled with Starkey, tearing his cutlass from his grasp. The pirate fled overboard and John followed. Tootles and Curly cornered Smee. Here and there a head bobbed up in the water, then there was a flash of steel, followed by a cry or a whoop.

But where was Peter Pan all this time? He was seeking bigger game.

Hook rose to the rock to breathe, and at the same moment Peter climbed up the opposite side. Neither knew that the other was coming. Each feeling for a grip reached out and found the other's arm. They raised their heads; their faces almost touched.

Quick as a thought Peter snatched a knife from Hook's belt and was about to drive it home, when he saw that he was standing higher up the rock than his enemy. That would not have been fighting fair. Peter gave the pirate a hand to help him up; and that was when the villainous Hook bit him!

It wasn't the pain but its unfairness that dazed Peter. It made him quite dizzy and twice the iron hand clawed him. But suddenly Hook was gone. He was in the water striking wildly for the ship, with his old enemy, the crocodile in pursuit.

The boys let him go as they scoured the lagoon for Peter and Wendy. But all they found was the deserted dinghy and they headed for home in it, confident the two of them would swim back or fly.

Once the boys' voices had died away, a cold silence came over the lagoon. Two small figures were beating against the rock. With a last effort Peter pulled Wendy out of the water and then lay beside her. He could see the water rising; he knew that if they stayed there they would soon be drowned, but he was wounded and he could do no more.

"Do you think you could swim or fly as far as the island, Wendy, without my help?"

But Wendy had to admit that she was too tired.

Then something brushed against Peter; it was the tail of

Goodbye, Wendy.

Michael's kite. Although Wendy clung to him and refused to leave without him, Peter tied it round her and with a "Goodbye, Wendy," he pushed her from the rock. In minutes she was carried out of sight and he was alone on the lagoon.

The rock was very small now and soon it would be under water. Peter was not quite like other boys, but at last he was afraid. A tremor ran through him, like a shudder passing over the sea.

But the next moment he was standing tall on the rock
with a smile on his face and a drum beating within him.
It was saying, "To die will be an awfully big adventure."

Seven

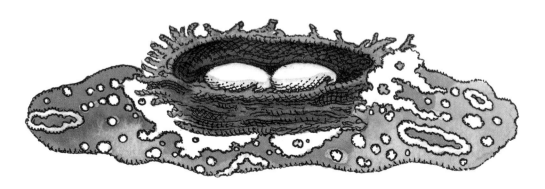

IS IT TIME TO GO HOME?

Steadily the waters rose till they were nibbling at Peter's feet. He looked out on to the lagoon and saw something white that he took to be a piece of paper floating towards him. But it was moving far more purposefully than that. It was in fact the Never bird desperately steering her nest towards the rock. She had come to save Peter, to give him her nest, even though there were still eggs in it.

Unfortunately the bird couldn't speak in any language that Peter could understand. She flew up, deserting her eggs, so as to make her meaning clear. Then Peter understood and caught hold of the nest. Looking around him he spotted the hat the pirate Starkey had left hung on a post. Peter took it now and lifted the two white eggs into it and set it on the

lagoon. It floated beautifully and the Never bird fluttered down upon the hat and once more sat snugly on her eggs.

She drifted in one direction, and Peter in another, both cheering. And even louder were the cheers when Peter reached the home underground – almost as soon as Wendy, who had been carried hither and thither by the kite. Every one of the boys had adventures to tell, but Wendy was so scandalised by the lateness of the hour, that she cried, "To bed, to bed," in a voice that had to be obeyed.

One important result of the adventure on the lagoon when Peter saved Tiger Lily from her dreadful fate was that the redskins became his friends. From that night on the braves sat up above, keeping watch over the home under the ground in case of a pirate attack, which could not be much longer in coming.

And so we come to the evening that was to be known among them as the Night of Nights. The redskins in their blankets were at their posts above, while, below, the children were having their make-believe tea. Wendy sat down to her workbasket with a heavy load of stockings and every toe with a hole in it as usual.

Shortly they heard a step above; Peter had returned bringing nuts for the children and the correct time for Wendy. The way you got the time on the island was to find the crocodile, and then stay near it till the clock struck the hour.

The children happily dragged him from his tree and all of them sang and danced as they had so often before, but never would again.

It was such a deliciously creepy song, in which they pretended to be frightened at their own shadows, buffeting each other on the bed and out of it; it was more a pillow fight than a dance. And then, at last, it was time for bed and Wendy's story, the story they loved best, the story Peter hated. Usually he preferred to leave the room when this story began, and perhaps if he had done so this time they might all still be on the island.

But tonight he remained on his stool; and you shall see what happened.

"There was once a gentleman," Wendy began.

"And a lady also," the first twin interrupted.

Wendy nodded. "They were called Mr and Mrs Darling. They had three children and a faithful nurse, a dog called Nana; but Mr Darling became angry with Nana and chained her up in the yard; and so all the children flew away to the Neverland, where the lost boys are. They knew, of course, that their mother would always leave the window open for her children to fly back by; and they stayed away for years and had a lovely time."

"Did they ever go back?" asked John.

"Oh, yes," said Wendy confidently.

But Peter uttered a hollow groan as though he were in pain. "Oh, Wendy, you are wrong about mothers. I thought like you that my mother would always keep the window open for me; so I stayed away for moons and moons and moons, and then flew back; but the window was barred, my mother had forgotten all about me, and there was another little boy sleeping in my bed."

Was this the truth about mothers? The toads!

"Wendy, let us go home," cried John and Michael together.

"Yes, at once," she said, clutching them. And without a thought for Peter's feelings she said, rather sharply, "Will you make the necessary arrangements?"

"If you wish," he replied as coolly as if she had asked him to pass the nuts. If she didn't mind parting, then neither did he. He went up to give instructions to the redskins to guide the children through the wood and then told Tinker Bell to take them across the sea.

The lost boys were gazing forlornly at Wendy and her heart went out to them.

"Dear ones," she said, "if you will come with me, I feel almost sure I can get my father and mother to adopt you."

When Peter returned they cried, "Oh, Peter, can we go?"

"All right," he replied with a bitter smile; and immediately they rushed to get their things.

But he had no intention of going with them. When Wendy gave them each their last dose of medicine, Peter would not take his. She saw a look on his face that made her heart sink.

"I am not going with you, Wendy," he said. Peter had no desire for a mother; he could do very well without one. He wanted to always be a little boy and to have fun. And to show that he didn't mind them leaving, he skipped up and down the room, playing gaily on his pipes.

When it was time to go the boys began to look doubtful, but Peter said, "Now then, no fuss, no blubbering; goodbye, Wendy," and he held out his hand cheerily.

"You will remember to take your medicine?" she said.

"Yes," he replied.

That seemed to be everything, and an awkward pause followed.

"Lead the way, Tinker Bell," said Peter.

But before they could move, the air above was filled with shrieks and the clash of steel. It was at that exact moment that the pirates chose to make their dreadful attack upon the redskins.

Eight

THE CHILDREN ARE CAPTURED

It was a dreadful attack because it was against all the rules. Everyone knows that it's always the redskin who attacks first and that he attacks just before dawn, when he knows the courage of his enemy to be at its lowest ebb. Hook, however, cared nothing for honour and what followed was more a massacre than a fight. Thus died most of the Indian tribe, though happily Tiger Lily and a few braves escaped.

The battle was soon over and in the silence which followed the children listened keenly to hear how their fate had been decided. The pirates, eavesdropping at the mouths of the trees, heard the boys ask Peter which side had won. And alas! they also heard his answer. "If the redskins have won, they will beat the tom-tom; it is always their sign of victory."

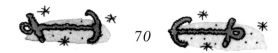

For Hook the night's work was not yet over; it was not the redskins he had come out to destroy, it was Peter Pan. He signalled Smee to beat twice upon the drum.

They heard the children cheer, "An Indian victory!"

Once more they said goodbye to Peter and climbed up their trees...straight into the arms of the awaiting pirates.

They plucked the boys from their trees and tossed them from one pirate to another, dropping them in a heap beside their captain. But a different treatment awaited Wendy.

Hook raised his hat to her, and, with chilling politeness, offered her his arm. He escorted her to the spot where the boys were being bound and gagged. All the boys were doubled up with their knees close to their ears like so many small parcels; but Slightly presented more of a problem; he simply would not fit like the rest. Every time the pirates tried to pack the poor boy tight in one place he bulged out in another.

Hook realised immediately that any tree large enough to fit this blown-up boy would also accommodate a man. His enemy Peter Pan at last lay at his mercy. He gave orders to convey the prisoners to the ship, while he remained alone.

Hook tiptoed to Slightly's tree, listened for a moment, then, hearing no sound from below, stepped in, and silently let himself down into the unknown. He arrived at the bottom of the shaft unhurt and peered into the room. In the dim light he made out the shape of Peter, fast asleep on the bed. Unaware of the children's capture, Peter had played for a while on his pipes, then lay down on the bed. He had nearly cried; but he knew how much more it would annoy Wendy if he were to refuse to take his medicine and to laugh instead, so he laughed a haughty laugh before falling asleep.

Thus defenceless Hook found him, one arm drooped over the edge of the bed. Hook stood silent at the foot of the tree, gazing on his enemy. Stepping forward, he found to his

fury there was one small obstacle: the door lock on Slightly's door was too low down for him to open it. Was his enemy to escape him after all?

But what was that? Hook's eye caught sight of Peter's medicine standing on a ledge within easy reach. Hook always carried about his person a dreadful drug. Five drops of this poison he now added to Peter's cup.

Then with one long gloating look upon his victim, he turned, and wormed his way with difficulty up the tree. As he emerged at the top he looked the very spirit of evil breaking from its hole. Muttering to himself he stole away through the trees, while Peter slept on.

It must have been not less than ten o'clock by the

crocodile when Peter sat up, wakened by Tinker Bell tapping on the door of his tree. She flew in excitedly and in one long unbroken sentence told him of the capture of Wendy and the boys.

Peter's heart bobbed up and down. "I must rescue them," he cried. As he leapt for his weapons, he spotted his medicine and thought of one thing at least that he could do to please Wendy. His hand reached for his cup.

"No!" shrieked Tinker Bell, who had heard Hook muttering to himself about the poison as he sped through the forest. She tried to warn Peter.

"Don't be silly, Tink. How could Hook have got down here?" He raised the cup to his lips, but in a lightning movement Tink reached it first and drained it to the last drop.

Peter, suddenly afraid, watched her reeling in the air; her wings could scarcely carry her to lie upon her bed. Every moment her light was growing fainter; and he knew that if it went out she would be no more. Her voice was so low that he could hardly hear it. In a whisper she managed to tell him that she thought she would get well again if children everywhere believed in fairies.

Peter cried out to all the children who might be dreaming of the Neverland, "If you believe, clap your hands; don't let Tink die."

Many clapped.

Some didn't.

A few little beasts hissed! But there were enough who clapped. Already Tink was growing stronger and soon she was flashing through the room more merry and impudent than ever.

"And now to rescue Wendy," said Peter.

When Peter rose from his tree a slight fall of snow had covered all footmarks and a deathly silence hung over the island. Even the crocodile passed by him without a sound. For a moment Peter hardly noticed that something was different about it: the crocodile had not been ticking. Its clock had at last run down.

Peter crawled forward like a snake, one finger on his lip and his dagger at the ready. Under his breath he swore a terrible oath: "Hook or me this time."

Nine

ABOARD THE JOLLY ROGER

The Jolly Roger lay at anchor, wrapped in a blanket of night. There was little sound aboard, only the whir of the ship's sewing machine, at which Smee sat busily working, and the occasional laughter of pirates sprawled over games of dice or cards. Hook walked the deck in a deep dark mood. He had poisoned Peter Pan, or so he thought, and was about to rid himself of the other boys. This should have been his hour of triumph, and yet the captain seemed profoundly miserable. The sound of his crew bursting into song was more than he could bear.

"Quiet, you scugs," he cried, "or I'll cast anchor in you. Are all the children chained? Then hoist them up."

The wretched prisoners were lined up in front of him.

"Now then, six of you walk the plank tonight, but I have room for two cabin boys. You, boy," he said, addressing John. "Did you never want to be a pirate, my hearty?"

John had to admit that he had once thought of calling himself Red-handed Jack.

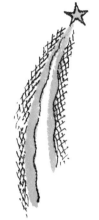

"And a good name too. We'll call you that if you join us."

"What would you call me if I join?" asked Michael.

"Blackbeard Joe," suggested Hook.

Michael was naturally impressed.

But John had another question: "Shall we still be respectful subjects of the King?"

"You would have to swear 'Down with the King!' " snarled Hook.

"Then I refuse!" cried John.

"And I refuse!" cried Michael.

"That seals your doom," roared Hook. "Bring up their mother. Prepare the plank."

No words of mine can tell you how Wendy despised those pirates. To the boys there was at least a touch of glamour in the pirate life, but all Wendy saw was that the ship hadn't been scrubbed for years. There wasn't a single port-hole on the grimy glass of which you might not have written with your finger 'Dirty Pig', and she'd already written it on several.

"So, my beauty," said Hook, "you are to see your children walk the plank. Have you any last words for them?"

Wendy spoke up bravely. "Dear boys, I have a message to you from your real mothers, and it is this: 'We hope our sons will die like English gentlemen.'"

"Now, tie her up," Hook shouted.

It was Smee who tied her to the mast. "I'll save you," he whispered, "if you promise to be my mother."

But Wendy replied, "I would almost rather have no children at all."

As the boys faced the plank they stared at it and shivered. Before Hook could give the order he heard a sound which stopped him dead.

It was the tick-tick-tick of the crocodile; coming steadily nearer. All eyes turned towards Hook as a terrible change came over him. He crumpled into a little heap and, with his eyes closed, he crawled along the deck. "Hide me," he cried hoarsely.

The pirates gathered around him, all hid their eyes from the appalling thing that was coming aboard. But the boys rushed to the ship's side to see the crocodile. What a surprise they got; it was no crocodile coming to their aid. It was Peter Pan.

The last time we saw Peter he was stealing across the island with a finger on his lips and his dagger at the ready. He had seen the crocodile and, realising that the clock had run down, decided to tick himself, hoping the wild beasts would take him for the crocodile and keep away; and he ticked superbly. What Peter had not foreseen was that the crocodile would follow him in the hope of getting back the thing it had lost.

Peter signalled to the boys not to give him away, then scaled the side of the ship, still ticking, and quickly vanished into Hook's cabin.

The pirates at last screwed up their courage to look around them.

"It's gone, Captain," Smee said, wiping his spectacles. "All's still again."

Hook drew himself up to his full height and cried, "Then back to Johnny Plank. But first, someone fetch me the cat-o'-nine tails. It's in the cabin."

The first pirate that strode into the cabin never strode out. There was a screech, followed by a crowing sound.

The boys recognised it, but the pirates shivered to hear it. In went a second pirate to rescue the first. Again came the death screech and again the crowing sound. And then a third. When Hook could find no other volunteers he seized a lantern and went in himself, but he soon came staggering out. "Something blew out the light," he said unsteadily.

Before he lost any more men, Hook hit on a new plan. "Lads, here's a notion. Open the cabin door and drive in the children. Let them fight the doodle-doo. If they kill him, we're so much the better; if he kills them we're none the worse."

The boys were pushed into the cabin and the door closed on them. "Now listen," cried Hook.

The pirates listened, but not one dared to face the door.

Inside the cabin Peter freed the boys from their chains and armed them. First signing to them to hide, Peter crept out to cut Wendy free. He whispered to her to conceal herself with the others and took her place at the mast, wrapping her cloak around him so that he should pass for her. Then he took a great breath and crowed!

The pirates, sure that all the boys lay slain in the cabin, were panic-stricken.

Hook tried to rally them. "Lads, I've thought it out. There's a Jonah aboard. It's the girl! Never was there luck on a pirate ship with a woman on board."

The pirates made a rush for the figure in the cloak. "There's none can save you now," they jeered at her.

None can save you now.

"There's one," replied the figure. "Peter Pan, the avenger!" And he flung off the cloak. "Out, boys, and at them!" he cried.

In another moment the clash of arms was resounding through the ship and a terrible battle raged. If the pirates had kept together they might yet have won, but they ran hither and thither in disarray and the boys soon scattered them further. Some tried to hide in dark corners until they fell prey to the boys' swords, others leapt into the sea. There was little sound other than the clang of weapons, an odd screech or splash and the voice of Slightly counting off the pirates as they fell, "Five – six – seven – eight..."

When all but one were accounted for the boys surrounded him, but Peter cried, "Put up your swords, boys, this man is mine!"

Thus suddenly the two came face to face.

"So, Pan," said Hook, "this is all your doing."

"Aye, James Hook," came the answer, "it is all my doing."

Without more words they fell to fighting, and it was closely fought. Hook's brilliant swordplay was more than matched by Peter's dazzling speed. Hook had the advantage of size and a longer reach, not to mention the dreaded hook, but Peter finally doubled under it and lunging forward pierced him in the ribs. At the sight of his own blood, which you will remember was the one thing he feared, Hook's sword fell from his hand. He was at Peter's mercy; even

now Peter invited the pirate to pick it up and the two fought again.

Hook battled on, every sweep of his sword would have sliced another opponent in two, but not Peter; he fluttered round him, continually blown out of the danger zone. Hook was tiring, fighting without hope, and now we have come to his last moment.

Seeing Peter slowly advancing upon him with dagger poised, he sprang upon the bulwarks and threw himself into the sea. Little did he know that his old enemy, the crocodile was silently waiting for him, jaws open wide.

Thus perished the infamous Captain Hook.

Ten

THE RETURN HOME

By two bells the next morning they were all up manning the ship, wearing pirate clothes cut off at the knee. I am sure you will guess who was the captain. Nibs and John were first and second mate. There was a big sea running and Peter calculated that if the weather lasted they would reach the Azores about the 21st June, after which it would save time to fly. Some of them wanted it to be an honest ship and others were in favour of keeping it a pirate vessel. Peter was every inch the captain and, once Wendy had altered one of Hook's suits to fit him, he almost seemed to take on some of Hook's cunning ways.

But let us leave them for a moment and travel on ahead,

back to that sad home from which the children had flown so long ago. Look, all is exactly as we left it: the beds are aired, the window still open, Mrs Darling sitting in the nursery, waiting for her children's return. The only change to be seen is that between nine and six the kennel is no longer there.

When the children flew away Mr Darling felt in his bones that all the blame was his for having chained Nana up in the first place, and that she had been far wiser than he. He had gone down on all fours and crawled into her kennel and promised that he would never leave it until his children came back. Every morning the kennel was carried with Mr Darling in it to a taxi cab, which conveyed him to his office, and he returned home in the same way at six.

How many times since has he told his wife, "I am responsible for it all. I, George Darling, did it"? But each time Mrs Darling has replied, "If only I had not accepted that invitation to dine at Number 27"; and each time Nana has thought sadly, "No, it was true, they ought not to have had a dog for a nurse." How many times have they sat in the empty nursery recalling every small detail of that dreadful evening until one or more of them has broken down altogether?

Little do they realise their children are even now within two miles of home. Let's see what they will find: Mr Darling, home from the office, is curled round in the kennel, his wife, as always, sitting in her chair in the nursery.

"Won't you play me to sleep," he asks her, "on the nursery piano?" and as she crosses to the day nursery he adds thoughtlessly, "And shut that window. I feel a draught."

"Oh, George, never ask me to do that. The window must always be open for them, always, always."

Mr Darling begs her pardon. Then, as she plays, he sleeps and while he sleeps two figures slip through the open window. Are they here at last? No, not yet. It is only Peter and Tinker Bell; they have flown ahead. What is in Peter's mind now?

"Quick, Tink, close the window; bar it," he whispered.

"That's right. Now when Wendy comes she'll think her mother has barred her out and she'll have to go back with me." Peter danced around the room with glee, then he heard the sound of playing and peeped into the day nursery to see who it was.

"It's Wendy's mother," he whispered to Tink.

The music stopped and now he saw that Mrs Darling had laid her head down and tears were in her eyes.

"She's awfully fond of Wendy," he said to himself. A huge struggle was going on inside him, for he wanted Wendy too, but they couldn't both have her. "Oh, all right," he said in a frightful temper. "You can have her!" and he unbarred the window.

"Come on, Tink!" he cried, "we don't want any silly mothers," and he flew away.

And so Wendy and John and Michael found the window open for them, and all seemed to be just as they had left it, but not quite.

"There's the kennel!" cried John, and he dashed across to it. "Hello, there's a man inside it."

"It's Father!" exclaimed Wendy.

"Surely," said John, "Father used not to sleep in the kennel?"

"Perhaps we don't remember the old life as well as we thought we did," said Wendy.

It was then that Mrs Darling began playing again.

"It's Mother!" cried Wendy, peeping in on her. "Let's slip into our beds and be there when she comes in, just as if we'd never been away."

 And so when Mrs Darling went back to the night nursery to see if her husband was asleep, all the beds were occupied. But she had seen the children in their beds so often in her

dreams that for a moment she couldn't believe her eyes.

Wendy sat up and cried, "Mother!" And all three of them slipped out of their beds and ran to her. Then Mr Darling woke to share their happiness and Nana came rushing in. There could not have been a happier sight; but there was none to see it, except a strange boy who was staring in at the window, watching them.

And what became of the other boys? They were waiting below to give Wendy time to explain about them; and when they had counted to five hundred they went up too. Of course Mrs Darling said at once that she would have them; Mr Darling hesitated. He considered six a rather large number, but he soon relented, and said that he would find space for them all in the drawing room as long as they fitted in.

As for Peter, he saw Wendy once more before he flew away. He didn't exactly come to the window, but he brushed against it in passing, so that she could open it if she liked and call to him. Mrs Darling came to the window too and told Peter that she had adopted all the other boys and would like to adopt him also; but when he learned that he would be sent to school and then to an office and would at last be a man he flatly refused.

"No one is going to catch me and make me a man," he said.

"But where are you going to live?" she asked.

"With Tink in the house we built for Wendy. The fairies are to put it high up among the treetops where they sleep at nights."

"How lovely," cried Wendy so longingly that her mother kept a tight hold on her. She made a kind offer though: to let Wendy go with him for a week every year to do his spring cleaning; and with this promise Peter went off quite happy again.

By the next year the other boys had gone to school and forgotten how to fly; they were already beginning to forget all about the Neverland and their life with Peter Pan.

But Wendy was waiting for Peter when he came to collect her. She flew away with him in the dress she had made from leaves and berries in the Neverland, and her one fear was that he might notice how short it had become, but he didn't.

She could hardly wait for all the thrilling talks they would have about old times and new adventures. This time she wouldn't have to share him with any of the other boys. They would have a lovely spring cleaning in the little house in the treetops, just the two of them; just Peter Pan and Wendy.